To the young people who are inspiring us
to take care of our planet home

—J. A.

For Jake and Natalie—
the little caterpillar and the precious butterfly

—R. C.

Henry Holt and Company, *Publishers since 1866*
Henry Holt® is a registered trademark of Macmillan Publishing Group, LLC
120 Broadway, New York, NY 10271 • mackids.com

Library of Congress Cataloging-in-Publication Data
Names: Alvarez, Julia, author. | Colón, Raúl, illustrator.
Title: Already a butterfly : a meditation story / Julia Alvarez ; illustrated by Raúl Colón.
Description: First edition. | New York : Henry Holt and Company, 2020.
"Christy Ottaviano Books." | Audience: Ages 5–9 | Audience: Grades 2–3
Summary: A too busy butterfly who spends her day hurrying and worrying
finds her own "quiet place" after learning about meditation and mindfulness from a flower bud.
Identifiers: LCCN 2019038493 | ISBN 9781627799324 (hardcover)
Subjects: CYAC: Butterflies—Fiction. | Mindfulness (Psychology)—Fiction. | Meditation—Fiction.
Classification: LCC PZ7.A48 Al 2020 | DDC [Fic]—dc23
LC record available at https://lccn.loc.gov/2019038493

Our books may be purchased in bulk for promotional, educational, or business use.
Please contact your local bookseller or the Macmillan Corporate and Premium Sales Department at
(800) 221-7945 ext. 5442 or by email at MacmillanSpecialMarkets @macmillan.com.

First edition, 2020 / Design by John Daly
The artist used watercolor, Prismacolor pencils, and lithographic crayon on Fabriano watercolor paper
to create the illustrations for this book.
Printed in China by RR Donnelley Asia Printing Solutions, Ltd., Dongguan City, Guangdong Province

1 3 5 7 9 10 8 6 4 2

Already a Butterfly

A Meditation Story

Julia Alvarez

illustrated by Raúl Colón

Christy Ottaviano Books

HENRY HOLT AND COMPANY

New York

In a field of many flowers lived a butterfly named Mari.

She spent her days flitting from flower to flower to flower, touching down only for seconds before she was off again.

If you asked her to name the flower she had just visited, Mari couldn't tell you. A daisy? A lily? A rose? An aster?

Everything was a blur in her hurry to gulp down nectar and pollinate the whole field. Sometimes she stopped for a moment, opening and closing her wings, but she wasn't resting. She was doing her wing exercises or going over her still-to-do list.

At night as she rubbed pollen off her tired legs, Mari could feel the ache in her wings and the speedy beat of her heart. She had definitely gotten a lot done today.

But had it been a good day?

She couldn't say.

"Go to sleep!" she scolded herself. "A lot more to do tomorrow!"

But instead of falling asleep, Mari counted the flowers left to pollinate; the days, hours, and minutes before she had to migrate; the mate she had to find; the eggs she had to lay.

Before she knew it, the sun was coming up. There seemed to be no time to rest. No time to enjoy just being a butterfly.

Her parents, the Posas, had never taught Mari to take her time. How could they? They had been so busy themselves, laying almost a hundred eggs, which had hatched into caterpillars, then grown into butterflies inside their chrysalises.

Before their children flew away, the Posas gave them some parting words. "We want you to be happy butterflies!"

"Can you teach us how?" Mari asked.

The Posas gazed out at the field filled with their children. There were so many of them that it was hard to keep track of who was who, and what each one might need to learn.

"Your instincts will guide you," Papa Posa pronounced confidently.

"Have fun!" the Posas called after Mari, waving goodbye with their wings.

One day, as Mari landed on a flower, her feet sank into the pollen, and the fragrant smell made her head feel light. She remembered resting quietly, wrapped in her cozy chrysalis. If only she could go back to that peaceful time . . .

"Hello, there." A friendly voice greeted Mari.
It sounded as if it were coming from deep inside her.

Mari looked left and right, up and down. Below
her in the sunlight, a bud was beginning to open.
Mari could see the white strip—like a smile—of a
bloom emerging.

"Do I know you?" Mari inquired.

"Ommmmm!" the bud hummed in reply.

Mari sighed with impatience. "Um, what?"

"Ommmmm," the bud repeated softly.

"Sorry, no time to talk. I've got a busy day ahead of me." Mari launched into her long to-do list. At last, she remembered her manners and introduced herself. Then she asked, "So, is your name really Ommmmm?"

"I don't have a name," the bud explained. "I guess for now you can call me Bud. But that will soon change. What's important is feeling happy just being who I am."

Mari recalled that special time inside her chrysalis. Is that what her new friend meant by feeling happy just being herself?

Bud hummed again, nodding in the breeze, as if he had heard Mari's thoughts. "Of course, back then you didn't know what you were doing. You were just following your instincts."

Papa Posa had used that very same word. Then, as now, Mari wasn't sure what it meant.

"Those instincts led you to become a beautiful winged creature who doesn't yet feel like a butterfly."

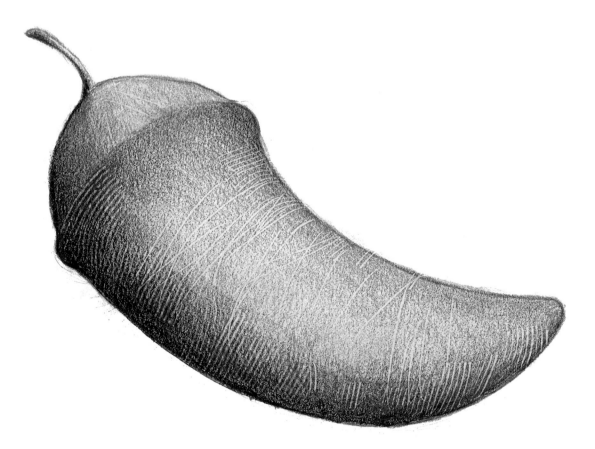

Mari had to admit Bud was right. She didn't feel like a beautiful winged anything. "I'm always so busy and sad, especially when I remember that peaceful time in my chrysalis." She wanted to cry, but her eyes didn't make tears.

"You can go to that quiet place inside you whenever you want."

Mari shook her wings. Impossible!

"Here, let me teach you how to get there," Bud said. "First, close your eyes."

"I can't!" Mari's eyes didn't have eyelids. "See? I will never, ever feel like a butterfly!"

"You already *are* a butterfly, Mari Posa. You just have to learn a way to get rid of the hurry and worry that keep you from knowing who you really are. That's what I'm going to teach you. Shall we start?"

Mari wasn't convinced, but it was worth a try.

"I want you to follow your breath."

She was about to ask what it meant to follow her breath, but Bud's voice carried her along.

"Imagine being inside your chrysalis, all soft and warm."
Mari liked imagining that she was back inside her
little home.

"Breathe deeply and slowly, in and out. In and out.
In and out. My, my, what a busy life you've had! First
as a tiny caterpillar, eating, eating, eating all those leaves,
shedding your skin every time you got too big.

"Next, you made a chrysalis, grew wings, and burst out into the world—all in a matter of weeks!

"But now, you can rest. There's nothing to do but breathe: In . . . Out . . . In . . . Out . . ."

Bud's words were soothing like a lullaby. But instead of putting Mari to sleep, they were waking her up to the sounds, sights, and smells around her.

Flowers were blooming everywhere: bluebells and purple asters and buttery yellow dahlias and dramatic black-eyed Susans. Had there always been so many kinds? Were their scents always so delicate and enchanting? How long had the crickets been serenading the field with their one-string fiddles?

"Breathing in, you are a butterfly. Breathing out, you feel happy," Bud chanted.

Mari joined in. "Breathing in, I am a butterfly. Breathing out, I feel happy."

And for the first time ever, from the tip of her tiny feet
to the tippy top of her curly antennae, Mari *felt* like a
butterfly! She spread her wings and fanned the air gently.
Before taking off, she bent down to say thank you.
   But Bud had disappeared.

In his place, a beautiful flower was blooming.

Mari reached down and took a dusting of
pollen to carry with her everywhere.

Growing Your Own Wings

While volunteering with my two young granddaughters at the Mariposa DR Foundation, an organization in the Dominican Republic that works to educate and empower impoverished girls, I realized that an important skill was missing from the many activities offered at the center. The girls were transforming into their winged selves, but given their youth, the lack of familial and social models, as well as the cycles of generational poverty in which they were caught, it was easy for them to get distracted and lose their way.

Julia with her Mariposas at the Mariposa DR Foundation.

Because I have been profoundly helped by my practice of meditation, I proposed to Mariposa's founder, Patricia Thorndike Suriel, that mindfulness training be added to the curriculum. Since the Mariposas already embrace the theme and logo of butterflies, that imagery could be used to teach the girls how to meditate.

While I wrote this story with the Dominican Mariposas in mind, I was also thinking of my

Julia with her husband, Bill, and granddaughters in front of the Julia Alvarez Library at the Mariposa DR Foundation Center.

two granddaughters, growing up in New Jersey under very different circumstances. They face the many challenges of young people in the developed world: distracting and overstimulating electronic devices, packed schedules that don't allow for time to slow down, and a flurry of social media threatening to turn them into social

butterflies with no true home in themselves. Additionally, young people everywhere are worried about the future of their home planet. More than ever, they need a quiet, centered space in which to feel safe and at home. Without that center, activism can easily morph into anxiety and loss of hope.

Julia teaches Mariposas how to fly.

Julia prepares a Mariposa for flight.

One evening, after a day of volunteering, I asked my granddaughters to join me in meditating. I told them a version of the story I've written down here, then guided them through this exercise: Sit comfortably, spines straight, breathing slowly, noticing your breaths, breathing in, breathing out, in, out. Silently review the memorable things you've done and felt today. Imagine a caterpillar: how it eats and eats and eats until it grows too big to fit inside its skin, then sheds it, grows another, and goes through this cycle several times. You too have many thoughts and feelings packed inside your mind and heart. Just notice them, thank them for their company, then let them go. Make room inside yourself for your wings to grow.

Breathing in, you grow wings; breathing out, you soar. In, grow; out, soar.

My hope is that wherever you find yourself—in a classroom, at the family dinner table, on the streets participating in a peaceful demonstration, or at home with a bunch of noisy, distracting thoughts in your head—Mari's story will be a useful reminder. May you too discover, as Mari Posa did, a quiet home inside yourself, no matter where your wings carry you.

Girls from the Mariposa DR Foundation and children from 3 Mariposas Montessori sit with Julia, watching Mariposas perform.

Mariposas meditating.